Witnesses of the Unknown

By
Morton Otwell Gourdneck

Preface

Dear reader,

As you journey into this book, you will read of a wonderful lady who possesses the most amazing gift. Just as her ancestors before her, she has inherited the ability to speak with the past and see into the present. You will learn of how her gift began and also of a very wicked individual, who had the same unique ability. When you have finished the story, if you have read carefully, you will also possess the ability to speak with the past and hear their stories. Use this wisely.

I feel I must warn you about the second story you will read. I have debated many weeks and gone against my better judgment, releasing it. You see, as I wrote this story, something tried to make its presence known to me. I hesitated to even finish it and often felt that I was not alone while writing it. I would honestly hate if this unseen presence showed up in your home while you read the story. So, as you read about a young man who brings a message back with him from the other side, please keep your lights on and make sure you are not alone in your home. Ol' Tripp may just be trying to tell you something, and believe me, you do not want to get involved. If this happens, close the book immediately and do not return to it.

The last story you will read, should you make it that far, is about poor Carrie Trainer, a sweet young lady, who soon learns how strong a mother's love can be, even from the other side. If you hear a loud rapping while reading this story, my wish for you is that it's only a friendly visitor knocking at your front door.

I do hope that you will enjoy these stories, as I can't seem to help writing them. If you should experience a visitor from the unknown, please let me know and I'll do all I can to correct the situation. It's the least I can do as I feel it truly would be my fault.

Thank you dear reader,

Morton Otwell Gourdneck

Ms. Mamie's Gift

"Union County officially has a creepy cemetery," Johnny Davidson thought, as he glared across at the old glowing white tombstones. Many of the stones were cracked and broken, but some were still intact as they sat within their family plots. Large trees shadowed the single stones, and sinkholes filled empty spots within the cemetery, revealing to Johnny that there were more graves than stones.

"I have to admit," Johnny said, " this is the first time I've interviewed anyone in a cemetery."

"This is the first time I've ever allowed anyone to interview me at all," Ms. Mamie Harlston replied. Her eyes were very kind and sparkled when she spoke. It was clear to Johnny that everything within her was good. She was an elderly African American woman with youthful skin and her words were comforting to him.

"I hope I can give you a good enough story for your magazine," she said.

"I'm sure you will, ma'am. I've heard an awful lot about you through the years and about your gift."

Ms. Mamie smiled as the two walked along through the headstones. She let her hand move over each one. Suddenly she stopped and knelt down beside a rusted metal marker. "It's okay," she said, as if she were talking into the air to someone. "I'm sure your daughter will bring your stone soon. Don't you worry now. She probably just has to get the money together. It will be here before you know it."

As Ms. Mamie stood up, Johnny looked at her with confusion. "Ms. Mamie, is everything okay? Were you talking to, um, someone?"

"Yes, that was Alice. As we were passing by she asked me when her daughter was going to bring her headstone. She was worried and said it should have been here by now. I told her it was probably on the way and not to fret. You know, some people go on, but some are still here walking around on earth. I've always felt that they stay near to their headstones or markers because it has their name and birth date on it. I think it helps them remember their identity and not forget who they are."

"Is Alice still here, listening to us now?"

"Oh no, she's somewhere else now. Maybe over by those trees," Ms. Mamie said, pointing towards a group of large cedar trees. "I have a feeling she's kind of a busy body."

Johnny began to jot down something on his notepad. He knew this was going to be the story of a lifetime. Ms. Mamie had always been looked at with admiration and also caution throughout her 90 years. People within the area talked of her gift, but not many ever saw her outside of her home.

"Do the dead frequently talk to you?" he asked.

"Oh my yes. They have ever since I was a little girl. I remember the first time I heard one speak. I was in an old cemetery right after my great grandfather's funeral. We were walking along to the graveside and I heard someone say, 'Leave this place!' I was only four or five years old and you can imagine how it startled me. I said, 'Who are you? What do you want?' Then I heard it again. It was a lady's voice and I could tell she was angry."

"Did you run away? I'm sure it must have been very frightening."

"No, not at all. I felt like something was wrong with the lady, like she had a story to tell me. She was needing somebody to understand her, so I came back the next day. The other kids, my brothers and sisters, they all went into town to get candy, but I came back out here to find that lady and see what was wrong."

Ms. Mamie stopped for a minute and looked to the sky. The sun was beginning to break through the clouds and she was trying to remember. A smile slowly spread across her face as she clasped her hands together.

"What I'd give to be a little girl again," she said with a laugh. "Ain't it good to remember back?"

"Did you find the lady's voice again?" Johnny asked .

"I did. She came out again and said, 'Ain't you scared?' I shook my head that I wasn't and asked her who she was. She was quite for a minute and said, 'Nobody remembers me. I didn't mean nothing to nobody while I was here.' I told her that couldn't be, she must have meant something to someone. She must have been good to somebody. She got quiet again and then I heard her voice coming from up on a hill and she said, 'Come up here.' I got up on the hill and I saw all these little tombstones. They were white and had lambs on top of them. I knew these were her children. All died at birth. Then I saw a tall white stone that had fallen to the ground. It had the name 'Mary' on it and said she died at age 32."

Ms. Mamie stopped and looked sadly towards the ground. "The poor girl, she died so young. She just felt like she didn't get to live any type of life. She wouldn't let go and move on. I told her she should move on, but they don't like it when you say that. It makes them angry. You shouldn't never tell them that."

"What happens when you ask them to move on? Do they?"

"They make some sort of noise. You'll hear it or see it when they do. It may be a tree limb crashing down, a stone falling over or a scream in the distance. They don't ever like to hear anyone say that. You be careful if you ever do."

Johnny smiled and jotted down a few more lines on his notepad. "I'm hoping I never get into a conversation with a, well, you know - a dead person." He said, chuckling and looking nervously at the ground.

"If you come to these places and stay long enough and just listen and read the stones, you'll hear one speak in some sort of way. It's not bad like you might think, especially if they know you have the gift. They can see it in you and they know they can approach you. There's a lot of good spirits still in this cemetery."

"Do you ever run into any bad spirits when you walk through the cemeteries?" Johnny asked. "I'm sure they're not all good are they?"

"Oh yes, there are the bad ones. You can tell them right away. They'll give you a feeling like when you see a snake. Your skin will crawl and the hair will stand up on the back of your neck, kind of like when it's cold outside. Most of the time, they did something bad when they were alive." Ms. Mamie pointed over to the other side of the cemetery and frowned. "Stay away from that side," she said. "I wouldn't dare walk over there. Some people died from taking too much medicine. They liked it but they died from it. I can hear them talking about it from time to time. They still wished they could get some and one of them was boasting about how she used to steal from people. They were bad and still are."

Johnny looked across at the newer end of the cemetery and got a chill as he listened to Ms. Mamie speak. He had that feeling before and wondered if he had been standing in the presence of evil spirits. Even though his hair began to stand on end, he didn't want to seem afraid so he continued on with the interview.

"Do you always become involved when someone speaks to you? I mean, do you always try to help or listen?"

Ms. Mamie straightened her long, silky, rose-colored dress and looked Johnny in the eye. He could see the sparkle in her eyes but the friendly smile began to fade and that comforting voice of hers turned to a stern and serious one.

"Mr. Davidson, I tell you, some of those folks still got serious problems, even though they're dead. They don't know what happened to them. They just don't know and I don't always have the time to help them figure it out. Sometimes I just walk away. It makes me sad but I just walk away. Around ten years ago, I was visiting with my family over in Johnson County and we went out to put a wreath on my great-aunt's gravestone. It had been very quiet and I hardly heard any voices at all out there. It was an old country cemetery, right out in the middle of some fields. It was dry that day and the fields had just been plowed. I watched two big dust devils blow right up to the edge of the cemetery. I just stood and watched them twirl."

"A dust devil?" Johnny asked .

"Yes, you know, you've seen them I'm sure. They look like a little tornado made out of dust. Not as strong as a tornado but they'll get you dusty if you walk through one."

"Oh, yes. I have seen those in the past. Did a voice speak to you through one?"

"No, this voice came from behind me. I heard her calling to me, she was a young lady. She said, 'What happened to me? What happened to me? Can you tell me why I'm here? Please I have to know! What's going on?' I looked forward and just kept walking, not looking back. Then, I heard her saying again, 'Please! Tell me what happened to me! Please! What happened to me?!' I turned around and saw it was one of those new kinds of headstones. It had the picture of a young white girl around 24 years of age on it. Right there, written on the headstone, were the words *Tragically Taken From Us*. I knew then it was a bad thing that happened to that girl. I just turned around and kept walking, walking towards the car. The girl kept calling to me and I wanted to cry because her voice made me so sad but I just kept walking. I didn't want to get involved, I didn't want to know what happened to her."

"I'll bet it is hard to walk away and not help everyone. Do you regret not getting involved with her and helping her know what the tragedy was?"

"Well, I'm still thinking about her today and that's been about ten years ago. I haven't been back out there and I always hoped that maybe she had moved on. Maybe she went to where she is supposed to be and is not afraid anymore. That's what I hope for her."

Ms. Mamie wiped a tear away as she thought about the girl. Johnny decided it might be a good idea to change the topic, even though he was still curious as to where her gift had originated.

"Ms. Mamie," he asked, "Are you the only one in your family who has ever had this gift? Were there others? Were the gifts the same? I know that some of the other families that I have researched seemed to have relatives who possessed special talents. Did you know that one person I interviewed could stop a person from bleeding and even cure warts just by whispering a secret to them?"

This brought a laugh from Ms. Mamie and seemed to snap her out of her sadness. "I have seen those type people before. Although none of my family could ever cure warts, they did have some special gifts. This gift all started with my uncle. His name was William. I remember him well. His eyes looked like they didn't have any pupils and he had an icy stare about him. When he looked at a person, he looked into their soul. People were always coming up to his house and asking him about things like where a lost mule was or some missing money. He'd look at em' with those eyes or look off towards the wall and go into a trance. When he'd focus back, he'd tell them what they needed to know. He would be right every time, too."

"Was William a fortune teller?" Johnny asked .

"People call them that these days, I guess, but he had something different than these people claiming to be fortune tellers today. He had a powerful gift and people knew it, too. When strangers got off the train, they'd be asking where 'William's house' was. One time when I was a little girl, I was playing over at his house. He was sitting on the front porch and a lady walked up and she looked ragged. Her eyes were black underneath like she hadn't been sleeping much. Her hair was sticking out and she had a sad frown on her face. She looked ragged I tell you."

Ms. Mamie let out a cackle and slapped her legs. "This woman looked so bad the dogs started howling when she walked up in the yard. Uncle William jumped up and started studying her right away. He told her to have a seat, she had come just in time, and he was going to help her. She sat down and started crying and he said, 'Now, now, I know things is bad but they gonna get better.' He grabbed her arm real quick like and I thought he was going to kiss her. I think she did too cause she kind of froze up and pulled back from him. He had her by the wrist and he took his other hand and started rubbing her forearm, round and round in a circle. Pretty soon, I saw a knot starting to come up on the lady's arm. The more he rubbed, the bigger the knot was. The lady's eyes were getting wider and wider as she looked at her arm. Suddenly, he reached into the knot and pulled out what looked like a baby loggerhead turtle. 'You good now,' he said to her. 'You was in a lot of danger though. Another woman is in love with your husband and she put a hex on you. I removed it though. You'll get some rest now; you'll have some peace.' The lady pulled out five silver dollars and gave them to him then she smiled and walked away. Uncle William gave me one of the dollars and handed me the baby turtle. 'Let this go in the ditch,' he said. ' That should be worth a dollar, huh?' I just laughed and told him 'Yes sir.' I let the turtle go and went back to playing but I never will forget him pulling that turtle from that lady's arm. It was something to see!"

Johnny struggled to keep up with Ms. Mamie's words. He didn't want to leave out a thing as he wrote. He knew he must be standing before a living miracle.

"Yes sir, Uncle William was a good man," Ms. Mamie said, looking at the sky and smiling. "The best that was ever made. But it's just too bad what happened to him. Nobody should ever have to go the way he did."

"How exactly did your uncle pass?" Johnny asked.

"Well, we'll get to that, Mr. Davidson, but you know, some folks in this world are evil, just plain evil. That's the way his oldest daughter was - Mentoria. She was really bad. I still remember the way she looked, all flashy and she loved her jewelry. She had the gift, too. It was a shame that such a wicked person had such a beautiful gift. She never used it for good either."

"Are you speaking of your cousin?" Johnny asked .

"Yes, Mentoria. That was her name. Uncle William tried his hardest to discipline that girl but there was no changing her ways. Even as a child, she was bad. She was about ten years older than me but I still remember the bad things she would do. I also heard my parents talk about how they had to hide the animals when she came over to visit. She was very cruel to them, even as a small child."

Johnny shook his head a bit and butted in. "You know, cruelty to animals is one of the early signs in most murderers or serial killers. I've seen the pattern in many of the articles I've come across."

"I wish we had known that back in those days," Ms. Mamie said. "It might have stopped a lot of hurt that came to my family and so many others."

"Is there anything specific you can recall about Mentoria? Any signs that you saw in the beginning that told you she might be a bad person who possessed a special gift?"

Ms. Mamie stopped at an old white headstone that was in the shape of an obelisk. Bending down, she took her smooth hands and brushed away the moss that covered the name and date of the stone. "Do you know what an obelisk is?" she asked.

"I know the shape," Johnny replied . "I've seen many of them around this cemetery and others I've visited."

"Well, it is a shape made up by the ancient Egyptians, it represents a ray of sunshine coming down from the heavens. It symbolizes the deceased person shining down on their loved ones. An obelisk would not be the proper stone for Mentoria. In fact, when she passed, I fought with several family members to keep from having an obelisk placed on her grave. And, to answer your question, I did see the signs in her. She was a very spiteful person."

"You don't seem to have very fond memories of her," Johnny said . "I'm a pretty good judge of character and I would think if you didn't like her, she must have been very bad."

Turning from the stone, Ms. Mamie began to speak but suddenly stopped as if to remember something. "I, I, remember in the 1930's. It must have been about 33 or 34, this girl's father passed away. He was a friend of the family and Uncle William brought his family to the funeral. The man who passed was a prominent business man, some people thought a lot of him but some didn't. Some even said he was a bit crooked, but Uncle William went to the funeral out of respect for him and his family. The man's daughter was about the same age as Mentoria and she was seeing this guy from school that Mentoria wanted to date. Mentoria had been bitter for sometime about this, so she walked up to her in the cemetery, just after they had lowered her father into the ground. The girl was walking away to go back to where her family was and that's when something evil happened. 'You know I see things don't you?' Mentoria said to her. 'You know I'm just like my Daddy and I saw your daddy in a dream last night, just as clearly like he was in front of me. He was burning in a fire and screaming so loud. He in a bad place. A real bad place.' The girl began to cry hysterically and fell to her knees on the ground, covering her face with her hands. Uncle William heard what was said and shouted out 'Toria!! Come here to me, girl!' Mentoria gave a wicked smile to the girl and walked over to him. 'What is wrong with you, Toria?! You should never say that to anyone!" She just looked at him as if she were trying to put him under her spell and said, 'But Daddy, I seen it. I seen it just as clear as day in my dream. I didn't say nothing that wasn't true.' Uncle William took her away from the others and grabbed her by the shoulders. He really got stern with her. He said, 'I know you did. I see those things, too, but you don't ever, ever tell the family things like that. It's not right. It's not good! What is wrong with you girl?!' Mentoria only smiled and said, 'Daddy, I promise I'll use my gift better. I won't do it again.' Uncle William let her go, but he seemed shaken. I can remember him pulling out his handkerchief and wiping the sweat off his forehead. That poor girl was still on the ground crying as the family tried to comfort her, and Mentoria stood beside a big oak tree smiling that wicked smile of hers."

"That was very cruel," Johnny said . His skin began to crawl as he thought of the incident.

"That feeling you're having right now," Ms. Mamie said "that feeling is because one of them is trying to talk to you. Mentoria was so bad that her evil still whispers in the air around these parts. You can feel that, can't you, Mr. Davidson?"

"I have to admit," Johnny said , "I have wondered about those feelings before. Maybe it wasn't just the chilly air, but something more spiritual."

Ms. Mamie laughed. "You know, you learn about death and the beyond all your growing up, but when you tell someone you feel or hear something from the other side, they look at you like your crazy. I never ask anybody to believe me. Believe me or not, I know what I know."

"Do you think Mentoria is still roaming the earth? That maybe she is with us here right now?"

Ms. Mamie looked around the cemetery as if she were trying to listen. She closed her eyes for a few seconds and then opened them again. Johnny noticed the familiar smile come back across her face as she began to speak. "No, maybe just her memory. Besides, I don't think any of the spirits that are here would allow her to be in this place. They wouldn't allow someone like her here."

Although the day was warm and sunny, a cool breeze came across the trees making the leaves rattle together. Ms. Mamie and Johnny looked up and noticed several sparrows flying from the limbs and out into the sky.

"You know," Ms. Mamie said , "I recall the day when a tragedy struck this community." Her eyes turned towards the ground and she almost sounded sorry that she had even brought it up but knew it was too late to take it back. Johnny paused as he steadied his pen and waited for her to continue. As she began to speak, the sparrows circled and landed back in the tree.

"There was a young man in town named Theaster. He had gone away to college and returned home to start a career and a family. He was a very sharp dressed man. I used to see him downtown certain days and he was always handing out money to us kids so we could buy candy and cokes. We all thought the world of him. He was a handsome man, too. He married a pretty young lady while he was away at college and had two children by her. We never saw her much, she mostly stayed at home and took care of the kids. But,

Theaster was always in town. He would come driving up in that nice, shiny, new car of his and pull out a pocket full of change to give to us. One day I heard from Mentoria's younger sister, A'Quillar, that Theaster had been having an affair with some girl in town. Some young girl had caught his eye and his wife had found out about it and left him, taking the children with her and moving to Chicago with relatives. Theaster realized what he had done and made a vow to go to Chicago and do whatever it took to get his family back. Everybody in town heard him say that." Ms. Mamie paused as if to steady her voice. It was apparent that she was becoming emotional. "Yes, he was a handsome man, a handsome man," she said, looking at the ground. "Mentoria thought that, too."

"I understand if you don't feel like talking about this," Johnny said, "I can tell it is a bad memory for you."

"No, it's okay. I think it needs to be said. So many people in my family have kept it silent for long enough. We all knew what really happened. Some men came to see Uncle William one day and the sheriff was with them. News had come that no one had heard from Theaster in several weeks. He had not been seen in town or Chicago either. The sheriff had formed a search team with no luck and they were now seeking help from Uncle William."

"Did the authorities often seek his help in these sort of cases?" Johnny asked, pausing from his writing.

"From time to time and only as a last resort. Uncle William was always willing to help, especially when families were hurting. In this case he told the men to sit down at the table with him and he looked off towards a wall in the kitchen with that look he had. He was in a trance for some time, and when he began to focus again, he cast his eyes over into the front room where Mentoria was sitting. He gave her an icy glare and she just smiled that wicked smile back at him.

He turned his head back to the men and said, 'Just up the river is a root wad. You have your men search in that root wad and you'll find Mr. Theaster.' The sheriff thanked Uncle William and he and his men left. And do you know what? They found that man's body right where he said it would be."

"Your uncle had been right? Did the man drown?" Johnny asked .

"Mr. Davidson, I tell you, nobody ever knew what the cause of that man's death was. They just never could tell but around his neck was a locket, a ladies locket. It was sterling silver with a red ruby in the middle. We had all seen a locket like that before, but none of us ever said a word about it. Uncle William had seen the locket in his vision, too. That is why he looked at Mentoria so hard when he focused back from his trance. It was her locket. We all knew what happened to Theaster but nobody ever said a word. Mentoria wasn't no more than 17 at the time of Theaster's death and she was already rotten to the core. She took what she wanted and if she couldn't have it, she did what was unholy. We should have stopped her. Uncle William should have done something, but that was his daughter, what was he going to do? What could he have done?"

As Johnny walked along with Ms. Mamie, he noticed he was beginning to feel more at ease. At first arrival, he had felt a little awkward being there but now it was as if he were accepted in some way. The stones no longer gave off an eerie presence but now seemed like large concrete books that told the life story of each person there.

"You feel welcomed here, don't you?" Ms. Mamie asked . "I can feel that in your spirit right now."

"Well, I do feel a little more comfortable than before."

"Like I said, if you listen, they will tell you their story and they will accept you. In life I have learned that it was never the dead people who gave me any problems, but the ones that are still alive."

"I guess you are right about that. Do you mind me asking you another question?"

"Well, you can ask, but you really don't have to. The answer is Yes, my Uncle William did know about my gift. That was your question right?"

"Yes, that was it. I can tell I'm going to have to be very careful about what I'm thinking around you," Johnny laughed .

Ms. Mamie reached down and placed her hand on a faded tombstone, allowing a black spotted lady bug to crawl onto her hand. As she looked it over, the sun beamed down on her hair giving her a bright glow.

"When I was about eight years old my Momma and Daddy took me to visit my other cousin, A'Quillar, at the hospital. She just got her tonsils out and we wanted to see how she was doing. When we got there, Uncle William was walking around in the hallway. I remember all those nurses dressed in white where buzzing everywhere. He was standing with his hands folded, pacing back and forth. Momma asked him if everything was alright. He told her that it was, but he was just bored out of his mind and ready to get out of that place. He asked me if I wanted to go for a walk with him outside, so I did. When we were walking through the hallway we came to the children's ward. It was quiet there and most of the rooms were empty. Uncle William stopped when we got close to the exit door. I stopped, too, and looked closely at the corner beside the door."

"Was something stopping you from going through the door?" Johnny asked .

"Well, I was surprised that Uncle William stopped and he was surprised that I had stopped, too. He looked down at me and said, 'Mamie, can you see that boy there in the corner?' I said, 'No sir' but I sure can hear what he's saying.' Uncle William looked at me surprised and said, 'Tell me what he's saying.' I said, 'That boy is wantin' him some ice cream.' Uncle William shook his head yes at me and said, 'Tell me that boys name.' I asked the voice what his name was and he told me. I looked at Uncle William and we both said 'Herman,' at the same time to each other!"

It had been many years since Ms. Mamie had recalled the event and joy spread over her face and tears streamed down her cheeks. Johnny snapped a photo of her expression, he knew it was real emotion, a feeling you only experience from being there. He wanted the world to see the look of joy on her face and wished everyone could know it at least once in their lifetime.

Ms. Mamie gave a sound of joy, a little shout of happiness as she clasped her hands together. "Uncle William was so proud at that moment! He grabbed me by the arms and said, 'Mamie! You've got the gift, girl! You've got it, too!' My eyes just lit up to know that someone, so well thought of by others, was proud of me. I felt real special. We walked along that day and he explained to me more about the gift and how it should be used and how it should never be used for bad, only to help others."

As Ms. Mamie stopped walking, she turned to Johnny and placed her hand over her mouth. "Oh my," she said, "You know, I just realized, the thing that has made me feel so special all these years has also made me feel so lonely and isolated. It is almost as if I have been cursed instead of blessed at times but also it is the only thing that gives me soundness. I'll bet that is the way my Uncle William felt too. I wish I could have told him that I understood. He would have felt good to know that somebody else understood. Maybe that is why he seemed so happy when he realized I had the gift, too."

"Did you become a favorite of your Uncle William after that?"

"I did, but we didn't talk about the gift in front of others. Also, he was careful not to show me too much favoritism in front of Mentoria. He knew she had the gift, too and he also knew of her jealousy and how it would put me in danger. Sometimes, when nobody else was around, Uncle William would say, 'Who you been talking to lately?' I'd tell him about the voices I heard and what they had to say to me. He would say, 'Mamie, just be glad you can only hear them folks and can't see them. Some of them folks are ugly characters.' We'd both die laughing when he said that."

"It sounds like you two had a special relationship. I also had a favorite uncle when I was growing up. I really do miss him. I guess we never really forget who is good to us when we were kids, do we?"

Ms. Mamie smiled at Johnny and patted his shoulder. "Kids are good judges of character. They can see inside a person and tell if they're good or not. I can tell you are a good man and I know your uncle probably had a lot to do with that."

" Thank you for saying that, I really believe he did," Johnny said, smiling.

"You know, no children ever went around Mentoria. She was older than most of us, but we didn't want to be around her anyways. My oldest brother used to say she was the Devil's girlfriend and even he couldn't stand her. She was always dressing up fancy and going out with boys all the time. If she did have anything to say to you, it was never nice. She was always being ugly to people, even her momma and daddy. Uncle William would let her get away with it, but not her momma, she'd snatch her bald headed if she talked back to her."

"I know you mentioned she had a sister, A'Quillar, was she like Mentoria. Did she have the gift, too?" Johnny asked .

"There was never a finer girl ever born on this earth as A'Quillar," said Ms. Mamie. "The exact opposite of her sister. She was more like an angel on this planet than anyone else. Always friendly and helping people. She looked after us kids like we were her own when we'd come for a visit. She was very pretty but had a large dent in her forehead. The family claimed it was an accident that happened when she was a child but A'Quillar told me that Mentoria had pushed a concrete cinder block off the top of the house and hit her. Sometimes she would be taken with seizers that lasted for a few minutes at a time. I think Mentoria was jealous of her and hurt her on purpose. I think everyone thought that, even her own momma and daddy, but they wouldn't say. 'It was just an accident' they'd say. As far as I know, she didn't have the gift. I think her kindness was her gift. I think that was far better than the ones we had."

"I can tell she must have been your favorite cousin just by your expression when you speak about her," Johnny said with a smile.

"Oh she was. She was not much older than me, but she always called me 'Baby' when she saw me. It was, 'Hi Baby, can I get you this. Or, Hi Baby do you need something else.' Sometimes I would just plum forget my name was Mamie when I was around her. She's still with us, you know."

"Is she now?"

"Yes, she's in a nursing home over at Cedar Hill, just by the Capitol. She's still taken by spells, but she inherited Uncle William's estate and has a lot of nice people to take care of her. When I go to see her, she'll just be sitting there smiling at me. The poor thing, she can't speak a word anymore but I can tell by that look, she still loves me and knows who I am."

Looking off through the cemetery, Ms. Mamie focused her attention on a faded white headstone. "Do you see that one there?" She asked.

"The one that looks like a tree stump?" Johnny replied.

"Yes, did you know that the stones themselves can tell you a story? There is a lot of hidden meanings in them. It's almost like a secret code. That is not just an old stump, it symbolizes something unique. Take a walk over to it and look at the inscription."

Johnny placed his notepad upon a headstone and made his way down to the old white stone.

"It's a young person buried there, isn't it?" Ms. Mamie asked.

"Yes, yes it is. It says here that they were only 24 years old. It says "Brother" on the stone. How did you know?"

"Well, take a close look at the limbs on the stone. Do you see how they look as though they've been sawed off? They are very short and close to the trunk. That symbolizes a life cut short. I know something else about a life cut short," Ms. Mamie said, looking off into the distance. "Maybe I shouldn't say, but I couldn't finish this interview without telling you all that there is to know."

"Is it about your Uncle William?" Johnny asked.

"Yes, it is about how he died."

"I have a feeling this was not a natural death. I can see it in your eyes, Ms. Mamie. Is this something you are sure you would like to discuss?"

"I think I'm ready. I've held it in for so many years and it's time to tell about it. You see, Uncle William was starting to have a time with Mentoria. She was getting older and harder to deal with every day. She just stayed and mooched off her momma and daddy even though she was old enough to get a job. She was constantly hurting someone, saying something nasty or just being plain mean to A'Quillar. One day, Uncle William came around the side of the house and A'Quillar was having one of her spells on the ground. Mentoria was standing over beside her and just a laughing. 'Look at you girl. Ain't no man ever going to want you. Look at how you jump around.' A'Quillar was foaming at the mouth and shaking violently, and just as Uncle William realized what was happening, Mentoria, kicked her in the side of the head. 'I aught to just go ahead and put you out of your misery,' she said. 'Ain't no man ever gonna want you.' Uncle William was so mad when he saw that, he grabbed Mentoria by the arms and shouted at her. 'Toria! What is wrong with you, girl?! Where is your compassion for your sister?!' And do you know what she did, Mr. Davidson? She spit right in her daddy's face."

Johnny gave a look of disgust as he quickly wrote down Ms. Mamie's words.

"Did, he do something about that?"

Ms. Mamie threw back her head and cackled as she recalled the incident. "He sure did, before he even thought about it, he raised back that big ol' hand of his and popped her right across the jaw! Mentoria went to crying and threw herself down on the ground. 'Why'd you go and hit me for, Daddy?! Why'd you go and hit me for?!' she screamed. Uncle William just walked over and tended to A'Quillar. When he seen she was fit again, he went inside to eat lunch and take his nap. Mentoria just lie there in the dirt, still bawling and squalling. I think it was the first time he ever really raised his hand to her in his life."

"Something tells me there is a little bit more to the story," Johnny replied.

"Oh yes, it was a Sunday afternoon and Uncle William settled in for his nap. He always like to get two or three good hours of rest after lunch. About midways through his nap, he woke up and called out to my aunt, "Ouch! Something pinched me!" She walked in to check on him and found him back asleep. She thought he must be dreaming and went back into the kitchen. A few hours later, she was starting to get worried and checked on him again. 'Get up, William. It's time for church. We're gonna be late if you don't get moving.' Uncle William didn't move at all so she jerked the covers back off him. Mr. Davidson, there under the covers sat a cottonmouth snake. My aunt went to screaming so loud that the neighbors came over to see what was wrong. My Uncle William was dead. Nobody knows how that snake got into the bed like that, but years later, A'Quillar told me that she saw Mentoria putting something in a jar that afternoon and going into the house. She couldn't tell what was in there because her vision was still a little blurry from her spell. When she told me that, we didn't say anything to one another, we just sat there quietly, but we both knew what was in that jar."

"Do you think Mentoria killed him?" Johnny asked.

"He bruised her ego that day, Mr. Davidson, and she had an ego two miles wide. She wasn't letting anyone get the best of her, not even her own daddy. That just shows you how cold and heartless she was."

Johnny noticed Ms. Mamie's clenched fist. He could tell she still harbored a deep resentment towards Mentoria. It soon loosened and that familiar smile spread over her face once more. "Mr. Davidson, did you get a chance to see Uncle William's stone? It's in the nearby Porter's Cemetery. People still come from all over to read it. Some even say it's haunted or they've received special powers after visiting it."

"I've heard of it and I do plan on visiting and getting a few photos. Doesn't it have an unusual inscription?"

"Oh yes, it talks about Uncle William and his God given powers and how he had helped and read into the souls of thousands of people in his life time. I guess that intrigues a lot of people. A headstone says a lot about a person. Did you know that some folks even come and take dirt from off his grave? They claim it will help them win at the lottery."

"I certainly look forward to seeing his stone, Ms. Mamie. I know it must be fitting for such a wonderful man as he was. Not to change the subject, but, what ever did happen to Mentoria, if you don't mind me asking? By what you've said, I'm getting the feeling that she died young."

A smile came over Ms. Mamie's face as she ran her hand along the rough edge of the headstone she was sitting on. "You know, I don't like to say that anyone is a mistake. We're all God's creatures, so I won't say Mentoria was a mistake, I'll just say that Mentoria MADE a lot of mistakes in her short life. She took advantage of men, she destroyed people's lives and enjoyed it, she even murdered and got away with it, but, in the end, she made the biggest mistake of her life. Mentoria always set her eyes on something that most others couldn't have. For some reason, the forbidden was just sweeter to her. If it wasn't meant to be had, she was going to have it and out of all the men in the county, she set her eyes on a young, up and coming preacher."

"A preacher?" Johnny asked. "I'm shocked."

"Not to say a preacher wasn't what Mentoria needed, but this preacher happened to be married with two children. She did all she could to sway him with her manipulations, no doubt it was a test to this young man. She was relentless, and just knew in her mind that she could break him down and get control over him. The preacher soon found himself torn between his service to God and his family or a life of sin, with a much younger woman. It is a choice he would not have to make, however."

"How is it that he didn't have to make the choice?" Johnny asked with a look of confusion.

"The preacher's wife made it for him. You see, Mentoria was politely asked to stay away from her husband. She denied that there was any sort of intentions of an affair and stormed away. The young wife knew better, she had a discernment from God and knew what a wicked person Mentoria was. One night, when the preacher was alone in his study, Mentoria made her way there to meet with him. What happened inside, no one knows, but on her way out, she was met by the preacher's wife and a razor blade to the throat. So ended the life of Mentoria and a precious gift that she did not deserve. People say that there are still blood stains on the sidewalk of that study to this very day."

"Was this long after your Uncle William had passed," Johnny asked.

"Maybe five years down the road. I can remember there not being anyone at her funeral except close family. I hate to say it, and forgive me if I sound cruel, but I felt as though an evil were gone from this world and a feeling of peace now took its place. Do you believe in Hell, Mr. Davidson?"

"I'm not sure. I've always heard that it is a terrible place. No one would ever want to spend eternity there. I guess the image I've always had of it is eternal suffering and torment. I haven't given it much thought though."

"Well, I have, and I will be so bold as to tell you that I think Mentoria is in Hell. I certainly couldn't imagine her any place else."

"I must tell you, Ms. Mamie," Johnny said, folding up his note pad. "This has been one of the most fascinating stories that I have ever been told. I can only imagine how the readers are going to react once it is published. I may have to come back and do a second story about you just to satisfy them."

This brought a chuckle from Ms. Mamie. "If anything has made me interesting in life, it is the gift. I am just an ordinary person with everyday thoughts. But, should the readers find me interesting, I wouldn't deny them a second story. I'm good at talking, I could probably come up with something to tell them for sure."

Standing up from her place on the stone, Ms. Mamie took Johnny's hand and tugged at it, signaling for him to follow her. As they walked along the cemetery pathway, she stopped at the foot of a large statue. It was an angel, white with black moss growing on the north side of it. The angel held out its hand as it appeared to be dropping a rose bud to the ground. The sky was now a silvery color and clouds began to form all around.

"I want you to listen," Ms. Mamie said. "Listen hard as you read the stone."

Johnny looked at the inscription on the stone. It was of a young lady who had passed away in the mid 1800s. A poem was written underneath her death date:

Life was but brief
For me.
I knew not love
Like many know.
Please do not forget
For I am not far
From you.
I will be waiting for you all
Just beyond that crystal sea.

"What can you tell me about this woman, just from reading that?" Ms. Mamie asked.

"Well, I can gather that she was a young lady who was very loved by her family. She must have felt the same for them. I gather she was not married nor did she have any type of serious relationship, due to her age. She would also want her family to go on with their lives, but never forget her as long as they lived. And I would believe her to be a very spiritual young lady as the poem makes reference to the Crystal Sea.

"In your mind, can you picture this young lady?"

"I really can, Ms. Mamie. That is amazing."

"If you were to see a picture of this young lady, I'm sure she would look just as you imagine. You see, her stone has told you a story. You have spoken today with someone from the past. Although you did not hear her voice, you listened and she spoke.

"I guess I never really though of it that way."

"One other thing, before we leave. You will always be welcome in this place. The spirits know you now. They know that you are not here to harm them and that you have taken the time to listen. You must also be warned. Now that you have listened, be careful who or what you listen to. Not all of them are good. Some are just confused, some refuse to leave, but some are very bad. You must learn to avoid them. Always pray for discernment, it is your protection. Now I must leave you and I thank you for taking time to listen to an old lady and her stories."

Shaking Johnny's hand, Ms. Mamie turned and began walking over the hill in the cemetery, back to her home, on the other side of town. As she disappeared through the stones, Johnny looked up and noticed a flock of sparrows flying from the trees. He knew this must be someone from the other side speaking to him. He listened closely and with a chuckle, said, "Yes, I will be back for a visit. It will be very soon and thank you for the invitation."

As he drove away in his car, the sun sat in the silvery sky and his mind began to focus on the amazing story that would soon come about. Looking back in his rearview mirror, he spotted the large white angel statue. There was now a dark shadow cast over, hiding it, but he knew in his heart that it held a story. He wondered if anyone else had ever stopped there to listen or if they ever would again. Ms. Mamie had taught him a secret - there was a story within the stones.

The End

Ol' Tripp

"I had a feeling you were going to ask me about him when I agreed to come down here," Toby Barret said, looking at the gentleman who sat across the room from him.

Professor Mark Groman stared back at Toby, studying his long beard and the bulldog tattoo on his shoulder. He seemed like a very good natured young man, a 'good ol' country boy' as most people would say.

"Well, you have to admit, Toby, it is a very unusual story. I don't think anyone around these parts has ever experienced anything quite like it before. Most people are wondering if you might even possess some sort of psychic abilities. Since this is my field of research at the University, I'm honored that you agreed to talk with me about your experience. Maybe we can make some headway on this subject."

"I sure as heck hope I can help. My momma never taught me anything but to tell the truth, so that's all I can tell you. You're not gonna have to hook me up to any wires or electrodes or anything are you?" Toby asked.

"No, not at all, but, as a starter, could you tell me a little bit about Columbus Tripp?"

Taking his hat off and slicking back his hair with one hand, Toby smiled and leaned back in his chair, recalling the past. "Oh man, I remember the first time I ever saw that dude. I was with an old buddy of mine and we stopped by a party, way back in the boonies. Some guy had a little makeshift shack and it was packed out with people. Not the kind of people a decent individual would want to associate themselves with, I'm talking backwoods misfits here. The music was too dang loud and they were playing this funky old song, 'Ain't Gonna Bump No More' I was cracking up listening to that. But, anyways, I spot one of the tallest, skinniest dudes I've ever seen. He's wearing this baseball hat backwards and has this long stringy hair hanging out of it. He had a little moustache where he hadn't shaved in a few days that made him look like a possum and the dingiest, yellow teeth I've ever seen. He wasn't wearing a shirt and I heard him say later it was because a police officer took it from him for what it said. It must have been some harsh stuff. I can remember thinking 'How weird is this dude?' So my friend walks up to him, pulls out a cigarette and says, 'Tripp, can I have a light?' This, lanky, possum looking, misfit of a human being looks him in the eye with the most serious look and says, 'I am the light. It is the flame in which you seek.' Then the dude just dies laughing with this shrill, unearthly laugh that actually startles me and makes me jump. I'm wondering what planet this guy just arrived from. I can tell he's having a blast, just being himself. People are high-fiving him as they walk by, patting him on the back and saying, 'Tripp, you the man, man! Where you been brother?' I look at my buddy and I'm like, 'Who is this character?' He tells me, 'That's Tripp. He's a legend around here. He's 42 years old and still partying hard. He can out drink, out smoke and out cuss anyone in this county. He's also been hitting the meth pretty hard lately, if you know what I mean?' I'd heard about the crystal meth, it was starting to become more popular around the boonies and I guess Ol' Tripp was kind of a pioneer at that time. I also remember he had this one girl, Heather, who was just hanging on him. He wasn't paying her too much attention, but she seemed like she was in love with him. If he took a step, so did she. I noticed Tripp had nicknamed her 'Shadow.' She looked almost gothic, in a redneck sort of way. Too much makeup and homemade tattoos, and she glared hard at any girl that crossed Tripp's path. He paid her no mind, though, and had a lot of love to give to everyone he saw. I just stood there thinking, 'Man, this is one unique creature.'"

"Did you develop a friendship with him right away?" Mark asked.

"We did start hanging out a bit after that. We were partying at a lot of the same places and we'd all pile into my buddy's truck and hit the back roads, drinking, spray painting bridges, frog gigging and all that sort of stuff. Ol' Tripp, he was up for just about anything. I can remember seeing this old Model T radiator in some guy's yard, way back in the boonies one night. I commented that I'd love to have it and thought it was so cool. The next morning when I woke up, I'll be danged it was sitting on my front porch. Tripp went back and got that mug for me. I just kinda laughed and hoped the cops never showed up looking for it. I still have it, but don't tell anybody."

"Ah, don't worry about that," Mark said with a chuckle. "This is all between us and I have no interest in causing any trouble for anyone. I just want to know more about this experience that you've had."

"I 'preciate that," Toby said, continuing his story. "You see, we were all getting pretty tight with Tripp, and it didn't take long to see that Shadow was really smothering him. Sometimes he acted like he was in love with her and then he was dodging her at every corner. One day he told us that he got a job over in Tennessee and was going to be down there for a while. Shadow went ballistic. She was begging him to take her, too. He kept telling her no but eventually, he gave in and said he'd pick her up the next morning and for her to be packed and ready. Anyway, he never showed up and she went off the deep end. She became almost dark in a way, kinda like she was mourning at a funeral or something. We only hung out with her because of Tripp, so we just stayed away the best we could while he was gone."

Toby's eyes suddenly shifted to Mark's desk.

"Something wrong, Toby?" Mark asked.

"You mind if I get a few pieces of that candy there?"

"Not at all, help yourself."

Toby reached into the glass jar and grabbed a handful of hard candy, unwrapping a few and tossing them into his mouth. "Thanks," he said. "I know I can't dip my snuff in here and the candy helps with the cravings. Anyway, I was telling you about Ol' Tripp taking that job in Tennessee. He never said what it was, only that he'd be making a lot of money. I expected him to come back home dressed up real nice, driving a new truck and high rolling. None of us could believe what we saw when he did show back up. It had been about three months since we'd seen him last, and he looked rougher than ever. I have seen him tore up before, too, but nothing like this. His hair was longer and looked like it hadn't been washed in months. He was trying to grow a beard but there were all these white blotches that wouldn't grow hair. I recognized them to be scars, like he must have been splashed and burned by something. He was even skinner, his cheekbones were poking way out and his bottom jaw was moving around a lot, like he couldn't control it. First thing that dude did, too, was ask me to let him hold a dollar. I could hardly believe it. I figured he'd be buying drinks for all of us."

"It sounds like he may have gotten involved in some heavy stuff while he was in Tennessee," Mark said. "Do you think he was up there learning how to cook the crystal meth? The way you described the burns, sounds a lot like what I've read in the past about meth lab explosions."

"There ain't no doubt about that," Toby said, unwrapping another piece of hard candy. "He went to work right away in an old shed that sat back in the deer woods. There were a lot of break-in's at the drug stores in town, too. Nobody in our group turned him in, but one day we were out at the shed and there were tons of empty packages that had the pills popped out of them. There were also a lot of matches with the tops broken off. We didn't really know what he was up to, but we knew it was something illegal."

"Most definitely meth," Mark replied. "Did Shadow know he was back in town?"

"Oh yeah, she was right on his heels again. He didn't want to hurt her; he was a good guy like that. He cared about people's feelings and all, but he was on a bad road. I think he just tolerated her, but it was obvious that she was deeply in love with him. I think she was into some bad stuff, too. She wore so much black makeup. That stuff was just caked around her eyes. We also noticed that she had a lot of scars on her arms. Some were long and faded and some looked like needle marks, when you got further up her arm. She really freaked us out. Have you ever had somebody just give you a bad vibe? That's what she did to me. One night she even came up to my buddy and told him that she and Tripp were going to be married in the spring.

We asked Tripp about it and he came unglued. 'It'll be a cold day before I marry that chick. I'd rather roll around in sawdust and pet a hungry beaver," he said, with that one of a kind laugh of his. Shadow was telling everybody that stuff though and even had a ring she was showing off."

Mark watched as Toby took more candy from the glass jar. It was quickly becoming empty.

"I'm sorry about that," Toby said. "Say, you wouldn't mind if I did dip a little would you? I know it's a tobacco free campus, but I'd probably do a whole lot better if I had a little pinch."

"Not at all," Mark replied. "Who's going to know?"

Mark watched as Toby took out a round roll of snuff from his back pocket and put a pinch between his bottom lip and gums. Grabbing a foam coffee cup, he quickly put it to use.

"I know this is a nasty habit but I've been doing it since I was a kid and can't seem to break it. I think I'll be able to talk a little better now," Toby said, spitting into the cup. "You see, Ol' Tripp, he got to making that stuff in his shed and I guess he was selling it around in the country like it was moonshine or something. People were buying it up as fast as he could make it. We were starting to worry about him because that's all he did. He stopped eating and sleeping and we'd go out and check on him from time to time, bring him food and what not. Well, I guess it was about the beginning of spring and we'd all decided to go fishing. None of us had seen Tripp in about two weeks so we thought we'd pick him up and get him out of that old shack for a little while. When we got there, it was a mess. Rotted food was everywhere and the chemical smell burned my throat. It didn't look like anyone had been there in a long time. No sign of Tripp anywhere. We looked around the area and nothing. No one in town had heard from him in a long time, and as a last resort, we even stopped by Shadow's house to ask about him. Let me tell you, when I saw her, I just about flipped out. This girl was wearing a bright yellow sundress, the kind like they wear on Easter. She didn't have on any of that dark makeup stuff and was smiling from ear to ear. I didn't even recognize her at first."

"Did she seem happy," Mark asked, studying the snuff that had now made its way onto Toby's beard.

"She was extremely happy. I'd known that girl for a few years and had never once seen her smile. She told me that Tripp had went back to Tennessee to make some money for their wedding and they were going to go on a big honeymoon trip. She said she had been working on writing the wedding invitations when we pulled up in the truck. We told her congratulations, but still took what she said with a grain of salt. We didn't think much more about it. We all knew she was a little out there in the first place and figured Ol' Tripp would show back up one day and we'd all have a good time laughing about it. Well, a few weeks went by and these two big ol' dudes from Tennessee showed up in town, asking about Tripp. They said they were business associates of his and were looking for him. They told my buddy that he owed them some money and hadn't been back to settle up with them. The biggest one of them told him, 'Tell Tripp that Big John Gardner and Hossfly came a calling.' They looked like they meant business, too. We were starting to worry and wonder if Tripp was in some serious trouble."

"Did you ever see Tripp again after they left?" Mark asked.

"Nah, he never showed back up. Every once in a while, someone would ask about him or we'd wonder where he'd got off to while we were driving down some back roads at night. I did see him again though. I guess that's what you are really wanting to know about, isn't it?"

"Yes, your experience," Mark replied.

Toby's huge arms began to shake a bit as he took a gulp, swallowing down a bit of tobacco juice. Mark could tell that this was not going to be an easy thing for him to talk about. Taking a deep breath, he took his hat off, once more slicking his hair back and quickly replacing it. "Alright, here goes," he said. "A few of us decided to go down to Memphis one night and take a walk around Beal Street. We were looking at the girls, listening to the music and just messing around. It was a pretty good night. I've had better, but we had a good time. It was Frank Ford, Terry Scolfield and myself; I'm sure you've probably read their obituaries already and know a little bit about them. We were heading back home that night and I was asleep in the back of Terry's car. I can remember them listening to this old song that used to be banned in the United States. I think they called it the Hungarian Suicide song or something. It got done away with because it was putting people under some kind of spell and they kept killing themselves. It was very depressing to say the least. Anyway, I drifted off to sleep and I heard this noise. I remember it was so loud, it reminded me of a tornado ripping through a building. I sat up in the backseat of the car and it was stopped. Both of the front doors were opened, and I saw Frank and Terry walking up ahead into this thick fog. I hollered out to them, but they couldn't seem to hear me so I opened my car door and started to follow them. When I stepped into the fog, I found myself in the weirdest freaking place I've ever seen."

Toby's voice began to shake a bit and he steadied himself. Mark noticed his tobacco cup began to move around as his arms shook with each sentence.

"Toby, do you need to take a minute? We can start this back up later if you'd like?"

"Nah, I guess I'll be okay. It's just that every time I recall that place, it seems so real and believe me, it's not a place I'll be going back to again. I'm getting myself right. I've been going to church every Sunday and Wednesday night and I stopped a lot of what I had been doing. The only thing I can't seem to shake is my snuff and maybe it won't send me back there. This is just a hard thing for me to think about, especially knowing Frank and Terry are still there and didn't get a second chance like I did. You wouldn't believe that place," Toby said, swinging his arms about and spilling a bit of tobacco juice on the floor. "It was grim, really grim. When I walked into that fog, there were tombstones standing everywhere, man. Not like the normal one's you'd see in a graveyard, either. Some of these were shaped like money, cars and even cheeseburgers! I started reading the inscriptions and they told about a certain person and how they died of greed, envy or even overeating. It was wild. I made my way around carefully, looking for my friends. I kept seeing them up ahead, but I couldn't seem to catch up with them, they were moving too fast. I headed down this dirt pathway through all these stones and I saw this red granite stone. It's real glossy and catches my attention. I put my hand on it to feel how cold and smooth the stone was and then I got the shock of my life - Ol' Tripp's face appears in that stone! I literally fell back to the ground!"

Mark scooted his chair in a little closer as he observed the seriousness of Toby's face. He had studied many cases of near death experiences before, but there was something different about this one. It was very real. Toby Barret was very real.

"Were you able to communicate with him?" Mark asked. "I mean, was he able to speak through the stone?"

"Yeah, he could speak, but he was trapped in that headstone. It was like I was looking at his reflection. When he saw me, he got real excited and frantic acting. He started yelling at me, 'Toby, I've gotta get some rest! She did this to me! She did this!' I had no idea what he was talking about, but he went on to explain his situation. 'I was a victim! She said she loved me and I was only hers. Go to 1375 Johnson Road, you know where she lives, man. I'm buried in her back yard under the sidewalk. I have to get some rest! You're going to get to go back. You're the only one that can help! Help me, Toby!'"

"I can't help but believe you, Toby," Mark said. "I honestly think you may hold a key here to the other side. I'm just not exactly sure where you were."

"Man, it wasn't a good place at all. Not one you'd ever want to see. I know Ol' Tripp was probably there for all of the things he did wrong, but maybe there was some hope to give him some sort of peace. He looked terrible. I sat there on the ground looking at him

and said, 'Trip, what can I do? I don't know how to help you. Tell me, man!' All of a sudden, he disappeared into the stone and it began to glow. It was almost like I was watching a big television screen as I looked at it. It flickered and scenes began to play out right before my eyes. At first, I saw Tripp. He was laying with his head in some girls lap and she was stroking his hair as he fell asleep. She reached under a pillow on the bed and pulled out a claw hammer. As I looked on, I could see her face. It was Shadow and she kept saying, 'We'll always be together.' Then, I saw Shadow kneeling down on her hands and knees, smoothing out a patch of concrete. That last thing I saw was Shadow sitting on her bed, filling out the wedding invitations. That's when Tripp's image flashed up again in the stone. He looked at me with these tired eyes, eyes that haven't seen rest in what looked like years, and said, 'Help me brother! She killed me! Give me some rest!'
When he said that, I just ran. I ran through the stones, falling ever so often. I didn't mean to leave him, I didn't want him to be alone and tormented, but I had to find my way out of that place. It wasn't somewhere I wanted to be. If there was a chance, I was getting out of there."

"Tripp seemed to know you would be able to leave. Did he ever say why?"

"No, I guess he'd seen enough people come and go through the stones that he knew who would go and who would stay. I sure tried to find my way out of that place. I walked higher up the dirt road and came to a marble mausoleum that had Ivy growing around the two columns in front. I pushed with all my strength on the doors and they creaked open. It was quiet inside, but I was still among the dead. As I walked along, I studied the room. There was a carpeted floor with headstones everywhere and coffins were set up like displays. Pictures sat on each one and told the story of the deceased. There were red satin sheets draped in each corner and candles everywhere. I read and studied the lives and deaths in the room. When I reached the back, I could sense the presence of pure evil. Whatever force was there did not want my help. In fact I could sense that it lived off of fear. The room had an organ that was playing by itself. Old pews and wooden folding chairs were set up everywhere. It smelled like a basement and the old books in the shelves were eaten with worms. The room started getting silent and the candles dimmed. I heard these noises that sounded like giggling and books started flying around the room. Chairs started turning over and the room was literally destroyed. All of a sudden, I heard a voice coming from a corner. 'Leave him alone! Leave him alone I said!' The chaos stopped and everything went back into place as fast as it started. It looked like the room had never been touched. Over in the corner, a small, old lady stepped out of the shadows. I recognized her right away. It was my old teacher from when I was a kid. She had been dead for many years. She gave me a stern look and said, 'I told them to leave you alone.' Then she disappeared back into the shadows. A door opened in the back of the mausoleum and I quickly walked out. A little ways up, I spotted a very peaceful hill. It had green grass growing and there were a lot of flowers laying around. The sun was shining bright and the birds sang. I had never seen such a beautiful place. I could see my family standing all around something. There was my father and mother and everyone I loved. I ran to them and shouted their names. 'I must be home,' I thought.

When I made it to them, no one spoke to me. I patted them on the shoulders, but no one even looked in my direction. They all hung their heads and looked so sad. I wondered why my brother was crying, so I pushed my way through their circle and looked at the ground. There was a big hole and they were tossing roses down into it. As I made my way closer, I looked inside. There I stood face to face with … Myself. The thoughts came rushing back and all of a sudden, I remembered. Terry and Frank woke me up with their screams and I sat up in the backseat. The headlights of an 18-wheeler were the last things I saw before I woke up in that awful place. Terry had hit it head on. The next thing I know, I hear some guy shouting, 'Clear! Clear!' And, I'm getting the heck shocked out of me by some paramedics. It was a long stay in the hospital, but I was alive! That's more than I can say for Frank and Terry. I miss those two, but more than anything, I morn for them because of where they are now."

"How long were you in the hospital?" Mark asked.

"Well, it was about three months. I had a lot of surgeries and then the rehab. But, I'll tell you, the whole time I was in there, what Ol' Tripp said to me was on my mind, day and night. The thought just wouldn't let up. It was almost like he was calling to me and I kept seeing those eyes of his, so tired and weary. I knew I had to do the right thing, but I didn't know if anyone would believe me."

Mark reached into his desk, pulled out a newspaper and placed it on the desk. There was a front page headline that read, "Local Man Solves Year Old Murder Case."

"I guess this is why I believe you," Mark said. "How could you have possibly known where to find Tripp's body? And, weren't you afraid the police might think you had something to do with this?"

"I was torn all right. That was my first thoughts, either they would think I was crazy, and maybe I was, or that I was involved with the murder. I just really didn't know if I should tell anyone or not, but leave it to Ol' Tripp, he wasn't going to let me rest until his murder was solved. One evening, during the summer, I was back on my feet a little bit and walking around. I saw Shadow out by the dam drinking with some people from the other town. I just got it in my head that I was going out to Johnson Road and take a look around. I drove my truck out there and went to creeping about in the backyard, looking at the flowers and what not. That's when I saw it. There was a new section of sidewalk about 7 foot long where an old piece had been busted out. I got the chills like you wouldn't believe. I knew that Ol' Tripp was laying right down there under the ground."

"Is that when you decided to go to the authorities?" Mark asked.

"You know how I told you I was trying to do better and all? And, well, I lied. I told the cops that Shadow had gotten drunk and told some people from the next town about burying him in her backyard. She couldn't prove it was a lie either because she WAS drunk or high most of the time and could have very well told someone. I had this old buddy that worked for the sheriff's office. We used to party together a little bit back in the day, so I told him about it. He knew I was a straight up guy and got a search warrant. I got to bragging a little bit about what really happened in the bars, later on. I guess that's why people think I'm psychic or have some special powers. You know how them old drunks can get. They like to stretch things."

"Were you there, when they dug up Tripp's body?"

"I was, and man, you should have seen the people there when they dug Shadow's backyard up. The officers kept yelling, 'Y'all get back! Get back!' It didn't do any good though, they just kept piling around the fence. Poor Ol' Tripp, he was right there where he said he'd be. When they found him, Shadow started screaming at them, 'Leave him alone! He's mine!' She even picked up a brick and threw it at one of the officer, just missing his head. Then she threw herself down on the ground and started crying. 'Now everybody's going to think I'm crazy,' she said. Well, duh, what just happened pretty much confirmed to us that she was. They cuffed her and actually had to drag her into the car. She scratched my old buddy up pretty good on his arms and the side of his face. I asked him later if he had to get a rabies shot."

Toby reached into his pocket and pulled out another pinch of snuff. "You want some of this? I'm sorry I didn't offer you any last time," he said with a serious look. "It's wintergreen. You may like the original flavor better. I tell you, it'll settle your stomach and put hair on your chest."

"Oh, no thanks," Mark said, fighting back a look of disgust. "You go right ahead though."

"Well, thank you, I believe I will," Toby said with a smile. "But anyways, like I was telling you about Ol' Tripp, after the autopsy, they buried him out at the Stranger's Cemetery. He didn't have any money and neither did his family. They were about as dirt poor as you could get so we put donation jars in every place in town. We only got about ten dollars from the bank, but you know what, we got nearly two thousand dollars from the old Donkey Barn. That's the tavern in town. Those guys loved Ol' Tripp. As much money as he spent in there over the years, I guess they felt like they owed him something. Plus, when dudes get to drinking, they get all sentimental and generous. We got enough money to get him a proper coffin and a little plot at the corner of the cemetery. It wasn't much, but it was better than being under Shadow's sidewalk, I guarantee you that. The funeral was one of epic proportions, too. They had a graveside service and all of Tripp's old party buddies were there. There were four-wheel drive trucks, motorcycles, four-wheelers, you name it. Everybody from the back roads to the back woods showed up. They made him this wicked looking thing to go on his grave. It was a deer skull fastened to a black iron post. It had all these little skull's hanging off it and a lot of people wrote a send-off message on it with markers. I was standing there while people were reliving old memories of him, and I got this feeling, just right down in my bones. I could hardly describe it, but it was so peaceful."

"Let me stop you right there, Toby. I've studied several of these experiences, and I want to make sure I don't miss anything. When there is closure in a situation, I've always heard about this feeling and I don't want to miss any detail of it. Please continue."

Clearing his throat, Toby reached into his bottom lip and pulled out the snuff with his finger, dropping it into his foam cup. "Well, I just felt like Ol' Tripp was really at rest. I'd go so far as to say he was saying 'Thank you, brother,' from the other side. I'm just a basic man, I don't think I have any psychic abilities or anything like that, but I knew that dude was talking to me, right there in the cemetery. I think he could see all of us and was truly thankful. It made me feel good."

"Toby, I think I have all the information I need for my research. This was truly a fascinating experience you had and I do appreciate you sharing it with me. I know it must have been hard to talk about at times, but maybe this will help others along the way, my friend. I promise to keep your name confidential in any papers that may be published on near death experiences."

Standing up, Toby shook Mark's hand and dusted some tobacco off of his jeans. "Hey, I was glad to do it, man. If you ever wanna know anything else, you just give me a call, brother. I'll tell you what I know. You know, I think when I leave here, I'm going to make me a trip out to Stranger's Cemetery. I need to go pay a visit to an old friend."

"I think that would be nice," Mark said with a smile. "Thanks again."

"Anytime. And remember, if you ain't got yourself right, now's the time to do it. You just come on down to our church anytime you get ready. Services are at 10 and 6 on Sunday and 7 on Wednesday nights. "

"I'll remember that. Thanks."

As Mark sat at his desk, he pulled up the online obituary of Columbus Tripp. Outside, he could hear the sound of pipes revving up on Toby's truck as he left the parking lot. He studied the photo attached to the obit with great interest. There was a mischievous darkness in Tripp's eyes. He wondered if he truly were at peace then got the feeling that he was not alone in his office anymore. As he glared more intently into the eyes of Tripp, there was a sudden flash of light on the computer screen and it faded to black. The electricity soon followed and Mark sat in total darkness, afraid to move. He jumped as his phone buzzed and quickly grabbed it from his pocket. The text he had just received was from "Unknown" and read, "This is what it's like. No peace here. Just darkness… Just darkness."

Placing the phone on his desk, Mark felt around in the dark and found his way to his office door. "Maybe it was just a wrong number," he thought, trying to rationalize what just happened. Although a grown man, educated to the highest level, fear gripped his soul and something seemed to be feeding off of it and enjoying it. Tonight was Wednesday night. Mark knew where a church was just down the street, and he was going to take Toby's advice and "Get himself right."

Dear reader, Have you gotten yourself right?

M.O.G

The End

A Mother's Spirit

"Do you think it's really wise to tell her? You know she's in a bad condition," Elizabeth Spence whispered, looking back into Miss Carrie Trainer's bedroom.

Carrie Trainer, one of the town's elite, had been sick for several weeks now. Although her doctor visited daily, her condition had only worsened and now she had taken to her bed.

"She has the right to know," Amanda Smith replied. "It's her mother. What do you think Doctor?"

Doctor Garrett rubbed his hand over the white whiskers that grew on his chin as he debated. "Ladies, I'm just not so sure it's a good idea. She's very near death herself, and if we break the news about her mother's passing to her now, she may lose all will to live. Let's just wait, at least for a bit."

"I agree," Elizabeth said, looking back into the room. "Look how restless she is. She's tossed and turned all night. She just can't take the bad news."

Studying Carrie's elaborate surroundings was a reminder to Doctor Garrett that death shows no favorites when it comes to social status. Her Victorian mansion was the largest in town and was filled with the finest decorations that old family money could buy. Imported Oriental carpets lined each hardwood floor and gold and brass fixtures hung from every wall, giving a certain class to the velvet chairs and couches within the rooms. While Carrie had experienced a most restless night, news had come from Virginia that her beloved mother, Beulah, had passed away suddenly.

"Carrie, Carrie," Amanda said, shaking her lightly.

Carrie focused her eyes and smiled. "Yes, Amanda. What is it?"

"Carrie, we have to go into town for a little while, but we are leaving you Amelia. She has agreed to come in to work today and take care of you. If you get hungry or need anything, please call for her. We'll be back soon. Try to rest, dear."

Carrie nodded and smiled as she watched Amanda leave the room. Soon, she could hear the front doors of the home close and she drifted back to sleep.

Amelia sang as she stood in a chair and polished the downstairs fixtures. She could never get used to the silence of the large house and singing always made her feel as if someone else were in the room with her. It was her "company" as she would tell others. Suddenly, she was startled by a voice coming from upstairs.

"Amelia? Amelia?" Carrie called.

Rushing upstairs, Amelia popped into Carrie's room and was surprised to see her sitting up in her bed.

"Yes Ma'am?"

"Amelia, I need you to do me a favor, please."

"Yes, of course," Amelia said, amazed at the newfound strength Carrie had gained.

"Amelia, I heard my mother, just out in front of the house. She was calling to me. She must have came for a visit. Will you please go out and bring her in to me?"

"Yes, of course," Amelia replied, unaware that Carrie's mother had passed away the night before.

Rushing downstairs, she threw open the front door, stepping out onto the porch. "Hello, hello," she called, looking around the front yard. "Is there anyone there?"

To her surprise, there was no one there and only the sounds of the sparrows in the large oak tree could be heard. Amelia returned upstairs and informed Carrie that she could find no one outside.

"But she must be there," Carrie insisted. "I heard her just as clearly. She said, 'Carrie, Carrie, I am coming for you, dear. I am here. I am here.' You must have heard her."

"I'll check again," Amelia said, with a look of worry. She quickly made her way back downstairs and looked outside once more. As before, no one was there.

Soon, Amanda and Elizabeth arrived back home and Amelia told them what had just happened.

"Oh dear," said Amanda. "She must be hallucinating from her sickness. I'll call the doctor right away."

Upon checking Carrie's room, they all found her in good spirits. "My mother came for a visit today," she told them. "I was very happy. I just hope that she will come inside soon to see me. She must have found something very fascinating out in the front yard to want to stay out there all this time."

Amanda and Elizabeth shook their heads and looked at each other. Amelia was now biting her nails as she grew nervous. Suddenly, there was a knock on the door and Doctor Garrett showed himself inside.

"Carrie, what are you doing sitting up in that bed?" he asked. "Now, you know you're supposed to be getting some rest."

"I'm waiting on my mother," she said with a smile. "She came to see me today. She's in the front yard."

Doctor Garrett quickly checked Carrie's pulse and blood pressure. He was looking her over very thoroughly and could find no worsening in her condition. "Oh, now," he said. "I think maybe you had yourself a dream. I was just out front of the house and there was no one out there. Maybe a few squirrels."

"But, Doctor, I tell you she was here. I heard her just as clearly as I am hearing you now. In fact, I think she is here now."

Everyone listened as the room grew silent. The candles on Carrie's nightstand began to flicker. Two loud raps were suddenly heard, followed by two more. Both seemed to be coming from within the wooden walls, then hair stood on end as all heard an unseen voice say, "Carrie, Carrie. This is your mother. I am here. I have come for you, Carrie. I am dead…"

No one moved for what seemed to be minutes. Maybe it was because everyone was afraid to move. Then suddenly, Elizabeth burst out in tears, "That was her voice!" she shouted. "It was Aunt Beulah! I'd know it anywhere!"

Carrie still sat smiling in her bed. "I'm here, Momma," she said. "I'll be right here."

"May I see you ladies in the hallway a minute?" Doctor Garret asked, standing up in disbelief.

Quickly and closely, the group exited Carrie's room and closed the door.

"I'm not quite sure how to label this event, ladies. I've never experienced anything like it. It's unexplainable!"

Elizabeth, who was still crying, grabbed Doctor Garret by the arm. He could feel her shaking from fear. "Doctor, I really do think we need to tell her. I think it's time," she said.

"Agreed," said Amanda. "Let's go back in and talk to her."

They entered the room and approached Carrie's bedside very carefully. "Carrie, we have something to tell you," Doctor Garrett said. "It's about your mother. You see, she passed away last night. She went very peacefully in her sleep. We just wanted you to know."

Carrie turned her head slowly and smiled at Doctor Garrett. "It's okay," she said. "I already know. My mother is here and watching over me now. I find great comfort in that, Doctor."

"There's not much more I can do for her now," Doctor Garrett said, talking with Amanda and Elizabeth in the front room. "I'll just keep an eye on her. Call me if you need me."

"Thank you, Doctor," Elizabeth replied, with tears in her eyes.

Over the next few days, Carrie seemed to grow weaker. Amelia had told several people in town about the strange occurrence and now many people were coming to visit and "Pay their respects." Most were only hoping to hear the voice of Carrie's deceased mother coming from the room. At the end of the week, Carrie had grown so frail, Doctor Garrett gave strict orders for no more visitors. Close family only.

"I just think the end is near," Amanda said as she opened the front door for Doctor Garrett. "She's just barely breathing and I can hear a rattling sound in her chest."

Making his way to Carrie's room, Doctor Garrett began to examine her. She was very weak and sweating from a high fever. Dipping a washcloth in a bowl of cold water, he wrung it out and placed it on her forehead. It was much darker in her room at night and everyone sat around her bed in the dim glow of the candlelight. Suddenly, a low, calming breeze blew through the bedroom window. The candles flickered and went out. All that remained was the red glow of their burnt wicks. Just as Amelia stood up to retrieve the matchbox, two loud raps came from the wall, just as if someone were knocking on a door. Everyone sat, frozen in their seats as two more raps were heard, this time much louder. Suddenly, the unseen voice was heard once more, "Carrie. Carrie. This is your mother. I am here in this room and I have come for you, Carrie. I am dead."

Doctor Garrett gulped as he heard Carrie reply, "I'm here, Momma. I'm ready to go."

Suddenly, two more loud raps were heard on the wall, and everyone jumped as Amelia struck a match and lit a nearby candle.

Doctor Garrett quickly made his way to Carrie's side and checked her pulse. Looking back at the family, his face and shoulders dropped. "She's gone," he said, sadly. "Gone to be with… her mother."

The End

Made in the USA
Columbia, SC
25 July 2022

63823200R00028